A NEW BARKER IN THE HOUSE

MORGIE, MARKIE + MOFFIE

Written and illustrated by

TOMIE dePAOLA

G. P. Putnam's Sons ⭐ New York

GLOSSARY

Hola (OH-lah) Hello

Pelota (pay-LOW-tah) Ball

Conejito (koe-neh-HEE-toe) Bunny

No juego (no hoo-AY-go) No play

Subibaja (soo-bee-BAH-hah) Seesaw

Tobogán (Toe-boe-GAHN) Slide

Columpio (koe-loom-PEE-oh) Swing

Hermana (air-MAH-nah) Sister

Hermano (air-MAH-no) Brother

Familia (fah-MEE-lee-ah) Family

¡Ay nanita! (eye nah-NEE-tah) Expression children use when they are scared

For Bob and Cathy Knight, dog trainers extraordinaire,
who brought "Markie" into my life,
my friend Alex and his *"FAMILIA,"*
and for Mario, who taught me to say *"¡AY NANITA!"*

Jennifer Smith-Stead, Literacy Consultant

G. P. Putnam's Sons, a division of Penguin Putnam Books for Young Readers, 345 Hudson Street, New York, NY 10014. G. P. Putnam's Sons, Reg. U.S. Pat. & Tm. Off. Published simultaneously in Canada. Printed in Hong Kong by South China Printing Co. (1988) Ltd. Book designed by Gina DiMassi. Text set in Worcester Round Medium. The art was done in transparent acrylics on Fabriano 140 lb. handmade watercolor paper. Library of Congress Cataloging-in-Publication Data   De Paola, Tomie.   A new Barker in the house / Tomie dePaola.   p. cm.   Summary: Twins Moffie and Morgie are excited when they hear that their family is adopting a three-year-old Hispanic boy. [1. Adoption—Fiction. 2. Brothers and sisters—Fiction. 3. Twins—Fiction. 4. Hispanic Americans—Fiction.]   I. Title.   PZ7.D439 Ne 2002   [E]—dc21   2001048128   ISBN 0-399-23865-4   10 9 8 7 6 5 4 3 2 1   First Impression

Moffie," Mama called.

"Morgie," Papa called.

"Come into the living room," they said.

"We have some wonderful news!"

Moffie was playing with her dolls.
"Coming, Mama," Moffie said.

Morgie was playing with his dinosaurs.
"Coming, Papa," Morgie said.

"Moffie, Morgie," Mama said. "You are going to have a new brother."

Moffie and Morgie looked at each other.

"Yes!" the twins shouted.

Moffie hugged Papa. Morgie hugged Mama. The family had been hoping to adopt a child, and now it was happening!

"He will be here in a few days," Papa said.

"Ooooh. A baby! He'll be so cute," Moffie said.

"He isn't a baby," Mama said. "His name is Marcos and he is already three years old."

"He comes from another country," Papa said. "So he doesn't speak English. He speaks Spanish. You'll have to help him learn new words. Won't that be fun?"

Yes, that did sound like fun. Both the twins were excited.

Moffie went to her room and sat down with her dolls.
"I wonder what he'll look like?" Moffie said.

Morgie went to his room and sat down with his
dinosaurs. "I wonder how tall he'll be?" Morgie said.

"I wonder if he's potty trained?"
Moffie said.

"I wonder if he can walk?"
Morgie said.

"I hope he can talk,"
Moffie said.

"I hope I can understand him,"
Morgie said.

Moffie and Morgie both began to think about what they could DO with their new brother.

"I'll show him how to have a tea party," Moffie said to her dolly.

"I'll tell him all about dinosaurs," Morgie said.

"I'll read to him—and show him my gold stars," Moffie said.

"I'll show him how to play baseball," Morgie said.

"I'll take him to school for SHOW-AND-TELL," Moffie said.
"I'll take him to school for SHOW-AND-TELL," Morgie said.

On Saturday the front door opened, and there was Papa with their new brother. "Moffie, Morgie, this is Marcos," Mama said.

"Hello, Marcos," Moffie and Morgie said.

"*¡Hola!*" Marcos said.

"He doesn't talk yet," Moffie said to Morgie.
"Yes, he does," Papa said. "Remember we said that
Marcos speaks Spanish. That's how he says 'Hello.'"

"Oh," the twins said. *"¡HOLA!"*
Marcos smiled. So did Mama and Papa.

"Okay, Marcos," Moffie said, taking over. "Come with me. We are going to have a dolly tea party."

"Now, I'm going to read to you," Moffie said. "I'm a really good reader." She pointed. "See all my gold stars?"
Marcos looked at the gold stars, but he didn't understand.

"Let me put these pretty baby clothes on you," Moffie said.
"I'll put you in my doll carriage with dolly and push you around," Moffie said.

"Potty!" Marcos said. He knew that word in English.
"Mama!" Moffie shouted.

"Come and see all my dinosaurs," Morgie said. They went into Morgie's room.

"*¡Ay nanita!*" Marcos yelled. He had never seen so many dinosaurs, and he was a little afraid.

"This is *Apatosaurus*, *Stegosaurus* and *Triceratops*," Morgie told Marcos. "Now, you say them."

Marcos didn't understand.

"Here is my baseball and bat. Do you want to go and play with Billy?" Morgie asked.
The bat was too big for Marcos.

"Potty!" Marcos said.
"Mama!" Morgie shouted.

It was time for bed.
"Mama, can Marcos sleep with dolly in her carriage?"
Moffie asked.

"Papa, can Marcos sleep in the cave with my dinosaurs?"
Morgie asked.

"No, kids," Mama and Papa said. "Marcos has his own bed and his own room."

So, Mama helped him put on his pajamas, and Marcos got into bed.

Morgie and Moffie ran and got lots of toys from their rooms.

They piled them in bed with Marcos. He was just about covered with toys.

As soon as Morgie and Moffie left, Marcos threw the toys out of his bed.

Now he had room to go to sleep. He kept his ball and his bunny.

Mama and Papa tucked him in.

Mama and Papa kissed him good night.

The next morning at breakfast, Morgie gave Marcos
a big spoonful of Morgie's favorite cereal—Dino Pops.
Marcos didn't like it!

Moffie gave Marcos a big spoonful of her favorite
cereal—Alphabet Bits.

Marcos didn't like it.

Marcos SPIT it all out!
"Mama!" the twins yelled.

"I know you are trying to be nice to Marcos, but maybe he doesn't like your cereal," Mama said.

"Here, Marcos." She gave Marcos a piece of toast with jelly on it, an orange, and a glass of milk.

Marcos liked them all.

"Mama, can I take Marcos for SHOW-AND-TELL at school?" Morgie asked.

"I want to do that!" Moffie said.

"I think we'll wait," Mama said. "Now, off to school, you two. Say bye-bye, Marcos."

"Bye-bye," Marcos repeated.

"Hi, Mama, we're home from school," the twins called.
Marcos ran and hid. *"¡NO JUEGO!"* he said.

"What did Marcos say?" Moffie asked.

"*No juego.* That means 'no play.' He's saying that he doesn't want to play now," Mama said.

"How come?" Morgie asked.

"Maybe Marcos wants to play other things," Mama said.
"Why don't you see what he'd like to do?"

"*¡Conejito!* Bunny!" Marcos said.
"*¡Pelota!* Ball!"

Morgie took Marcos and his bunny down the slide.

Moffie put Marcos on the swing and pushed him gently.

Moffie took Marcos and his bunny on the seesaw.

Morgie rolled the ball back and forth with Marcos.

That night the family sat down for dinner together.
Marcos pointed at himself and said, "Me. Markie."
Then he pointed at Moffie and Morgie.
"*Hermana*—sister. *Hermano*—brother," Marcos said.
Moffie and Morgie smiled.
They pointed at Marcos.
"Markie," they said. "*Hermano*—brother!"

"*Familia*," Mama and Papa said. "FAMILY!"